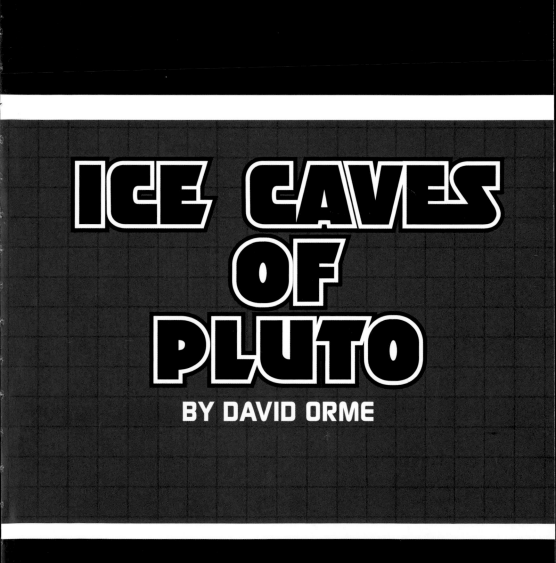

ICE CAVES OF PLUTO

BY DAVID ORME

STONE ARCH BOOKS
www.stonearchbooks.com

First published in the United States in 2009
by Stone Arch Books
151 Good Counsel Drive, P.O. Box 669
Mankato, Minnesota 56002
www.stonearchbooks.com

Library of Congress Cataloging-in-Publication Data
Orme, David, 1948 Mar. 1–
    [Boffin Boy and the Ice Caves of Pluto]
    Ice Caves of Pluto / by David Orme; illustrated by Peter Richardson.
    p. cm. — (Billy Blaster)
    Orginally published: Boffin Boy and the Ice Caves of Pluto. Watlington:
Ransom, 2007.
    ISBN 978-1-4342-1275-7 (library binding)
    1. Graphic novels. [1. Graphic novels. 2. Heroes—Fiction. 3. Science fiction.]
I. Richardson, Peter, 1965– ill. II. Title.
PZ7.7.O76Ice 2009
741.5'973—dc22   2008031379

Summary:
Billy Blaster travels to Pluto with his friend Wu Hoo. Things really get interesting when
Billy finds an alien ship trapped under the ice. Inside, he finds his alien friends, the
Snurgons, frozen stiff! Can Billy free the Snurgon ship, save his friends, and find a way out
of the ice caves of Pluto?

Creative Director: Heather Kindseth
Graphic Designer: Carla Zetina-Yglesias

1 2 3 4 5 6 14 13 12 11 10 09

BILLY BLASTER

written by
DAVID ORME

illustrated by
PETER RICHARDSON

ICE CAVES OF PLUTO

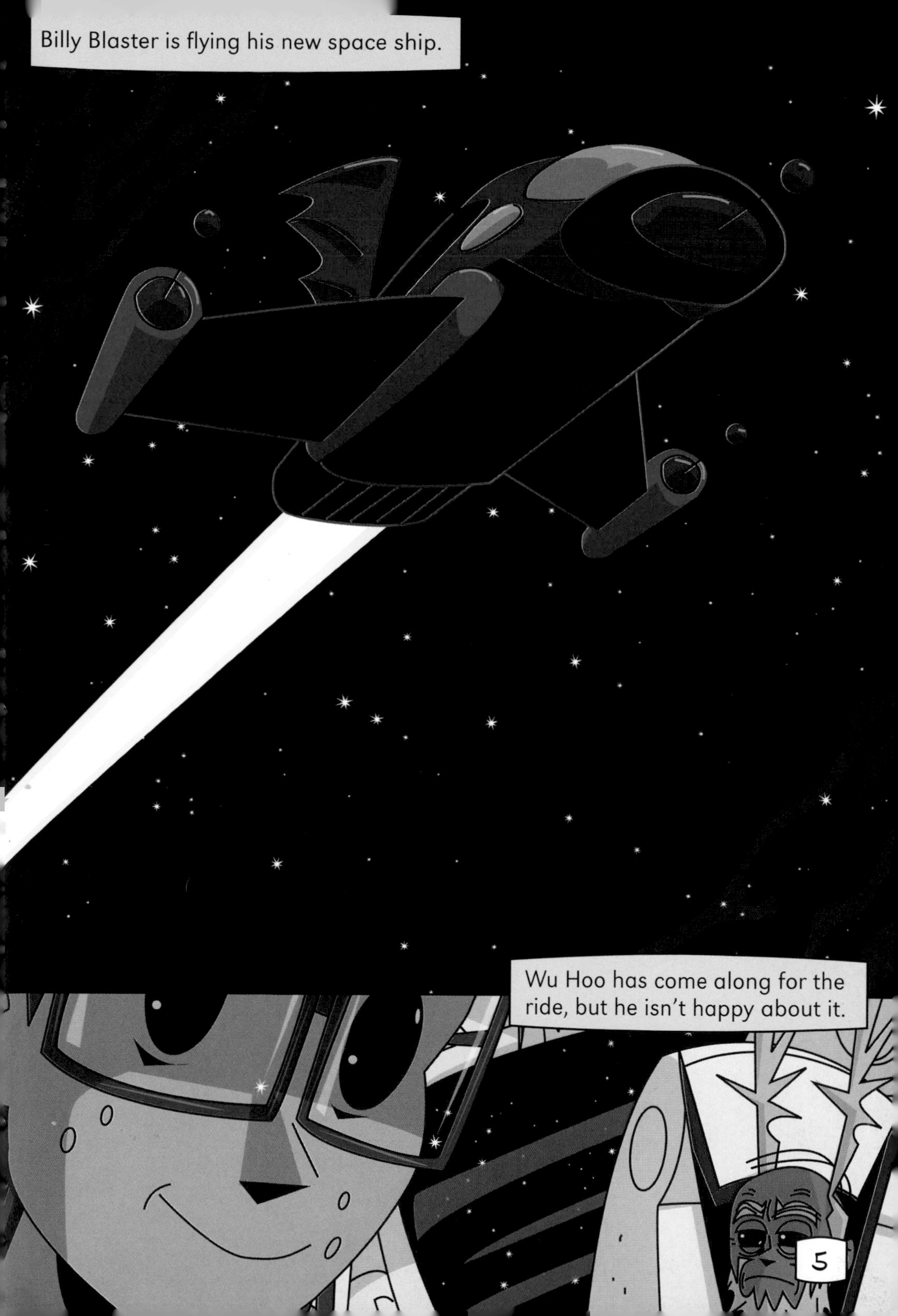
Billy Blaster is flying his new space ship.
Wu Hoo has come along for the ride, but he isn't happy about it.

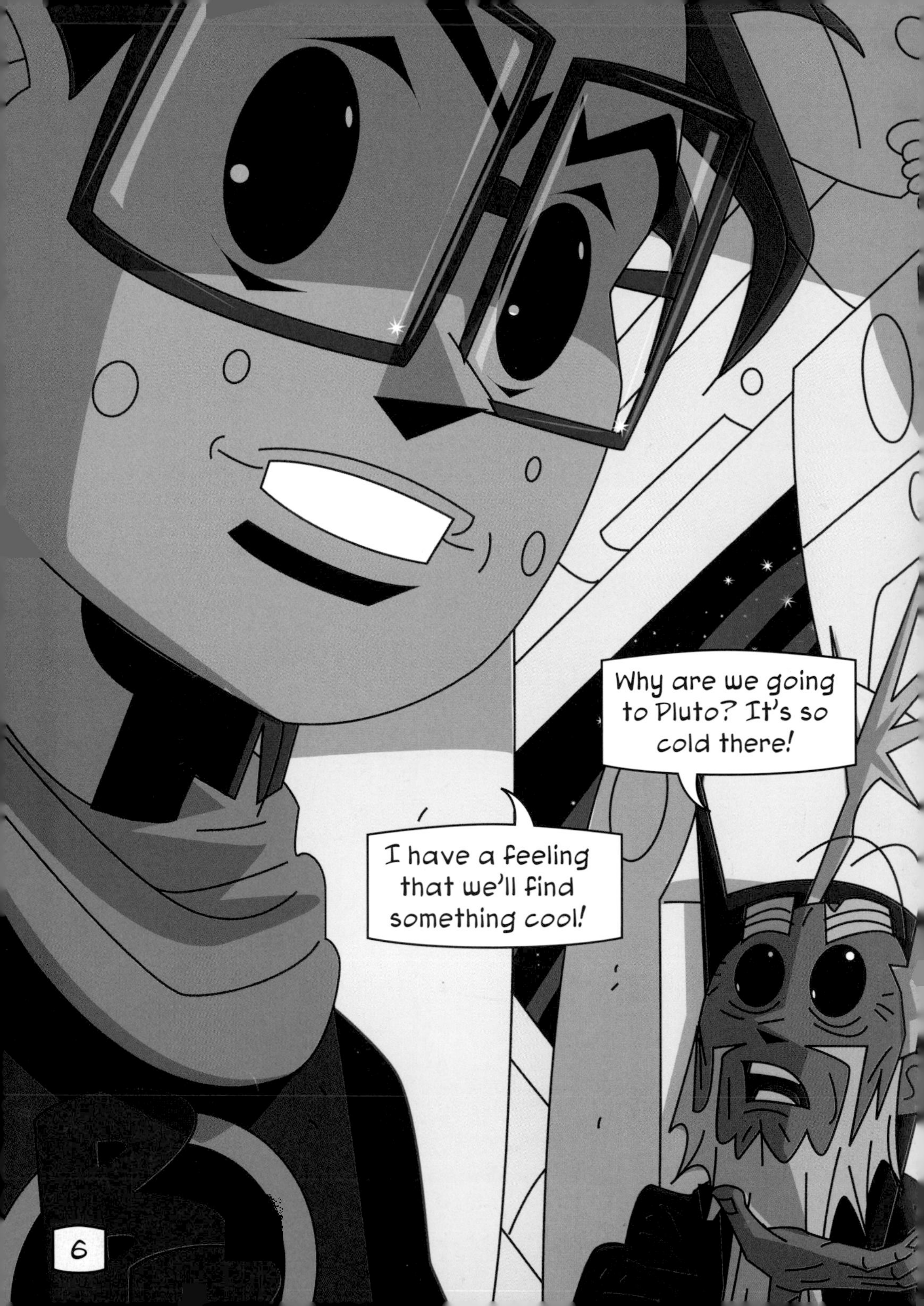
Why are we going to Pluto? It's so cold there!
I have a feeling that we'll find something cool!

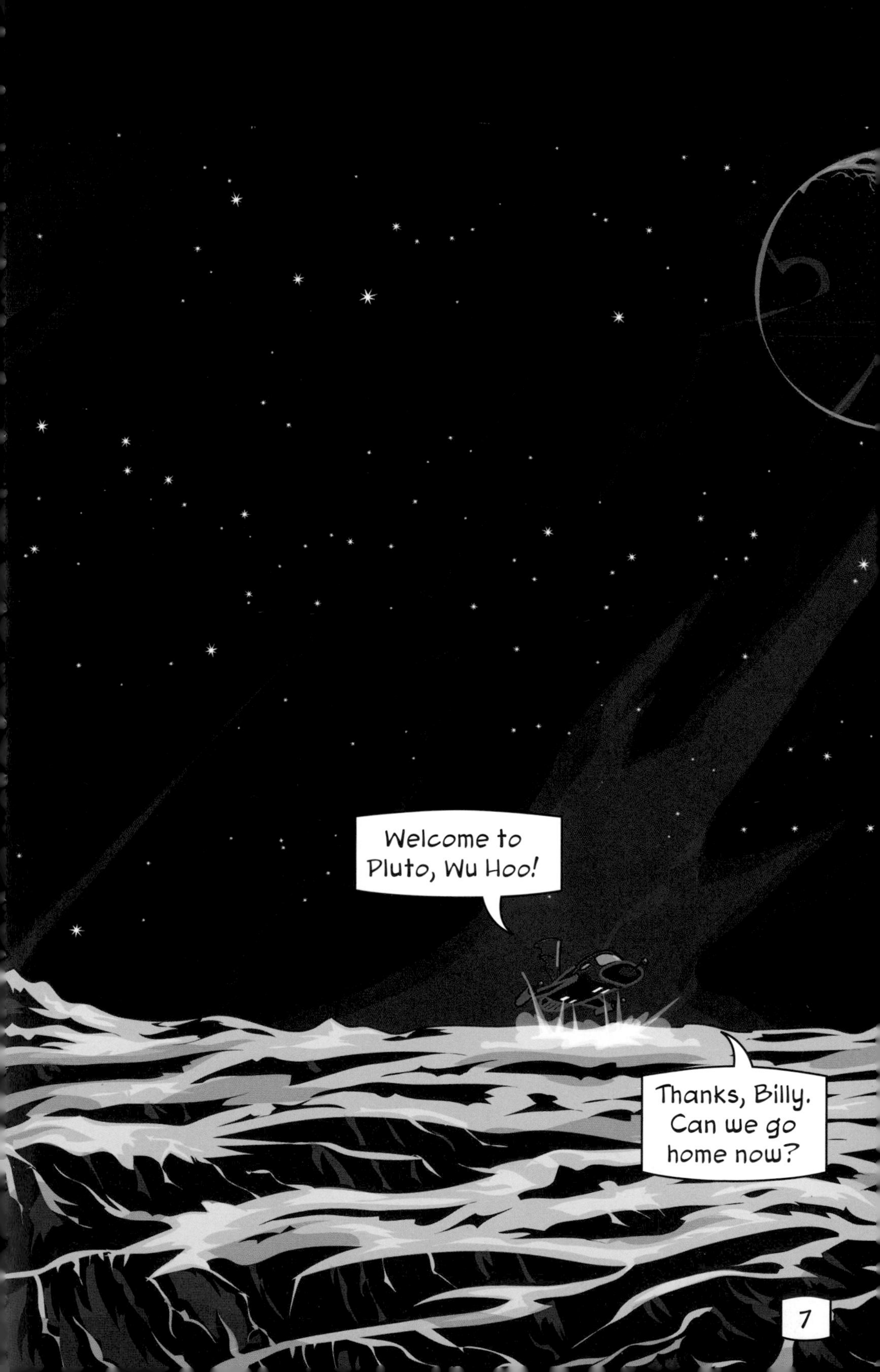
Welcome to Pluto, Wu Hoo!
Thanks, Billy. Can we go home now?

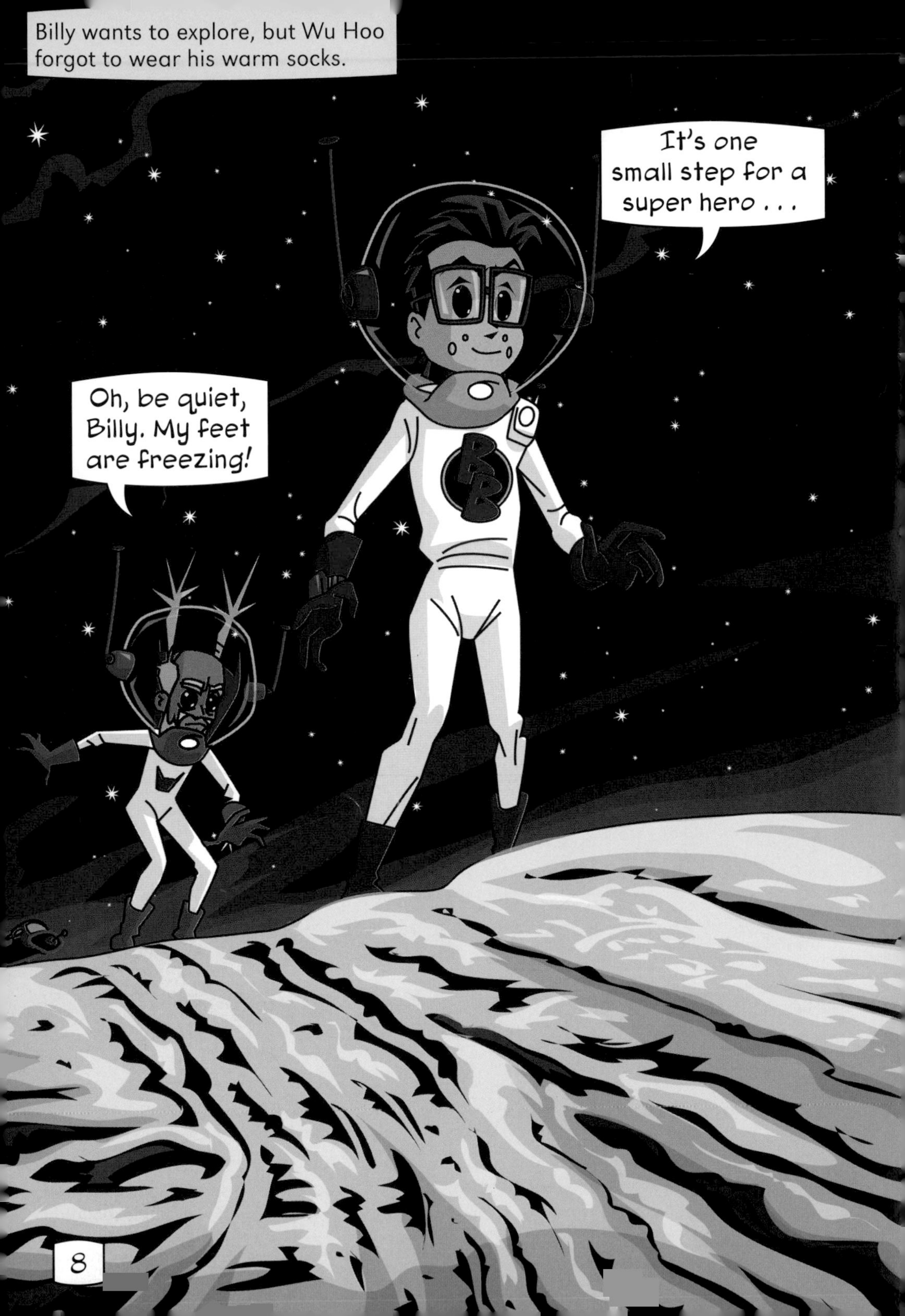
Billy wants to explore, but Wu Hoo forgot to wear his warm socks.
It's one small step for a super hero . . .
Oh, be quiet, Billy. My feet are freezing!

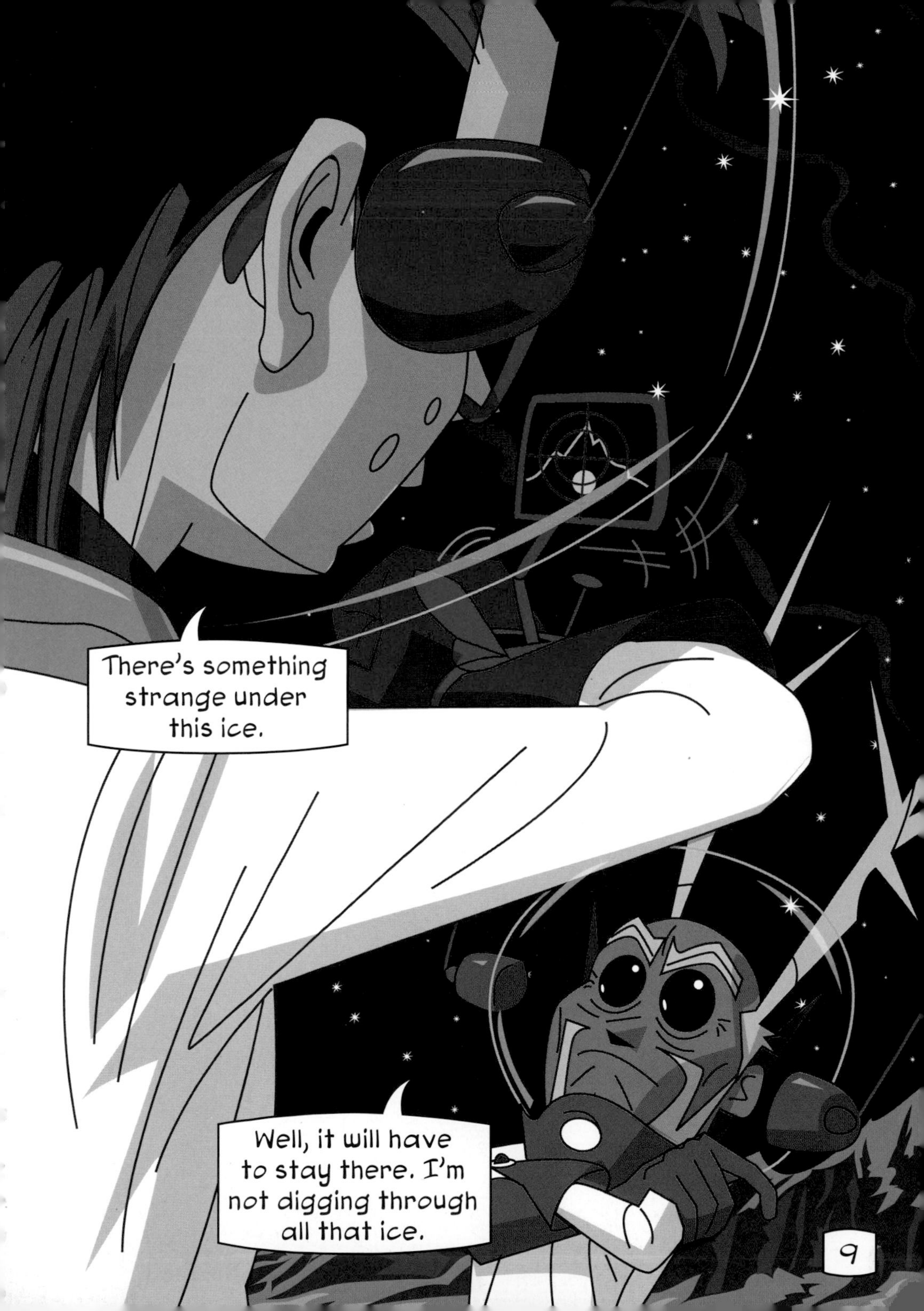
There's something strange under this ice.
Well, it will have to stay there. I'm not digging through all that ice.

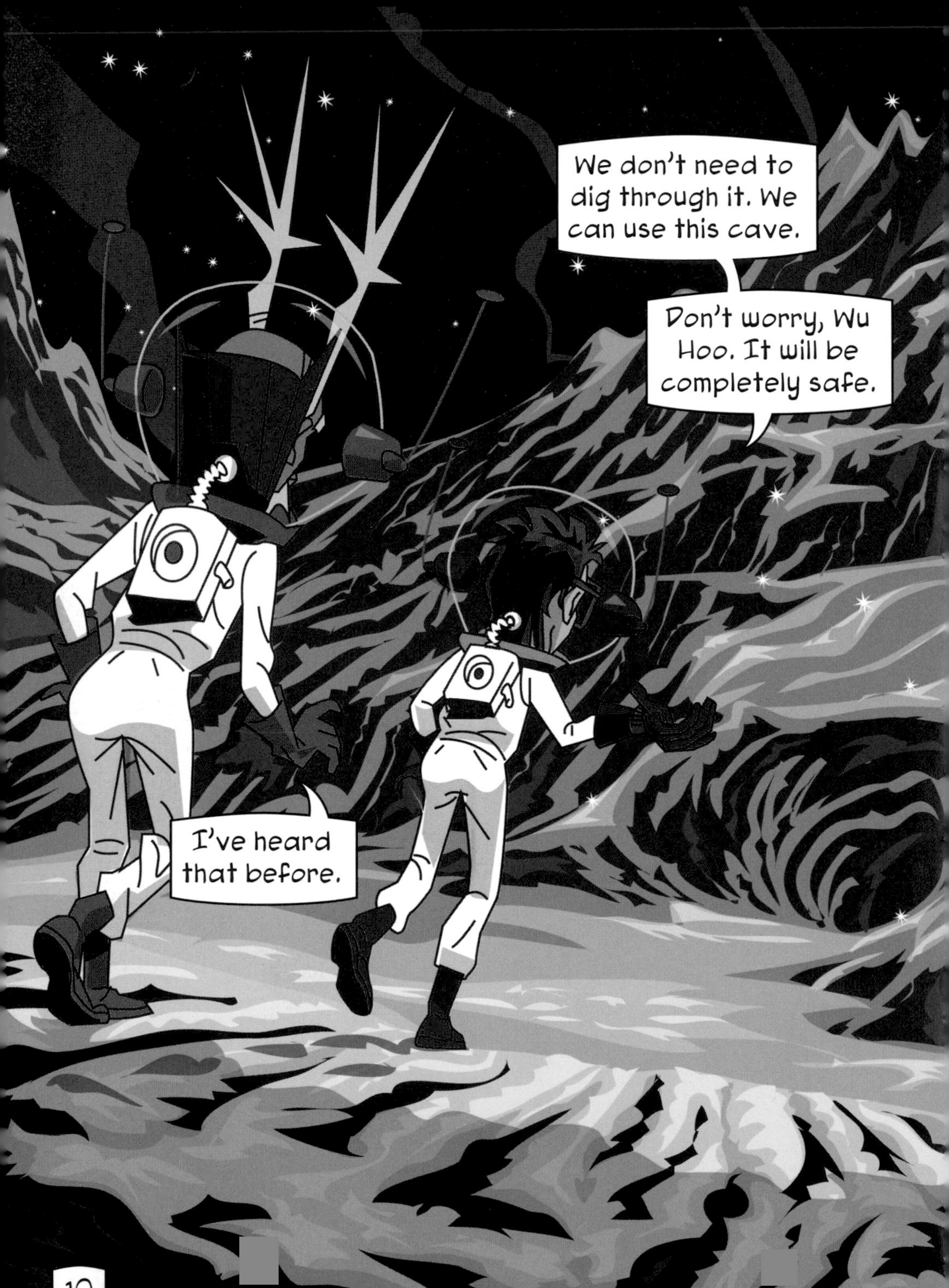
We don't need to dig through it. We can use this cave.
Don't worry, Wu Hoo. It will be completely safe.
I've heard that before.

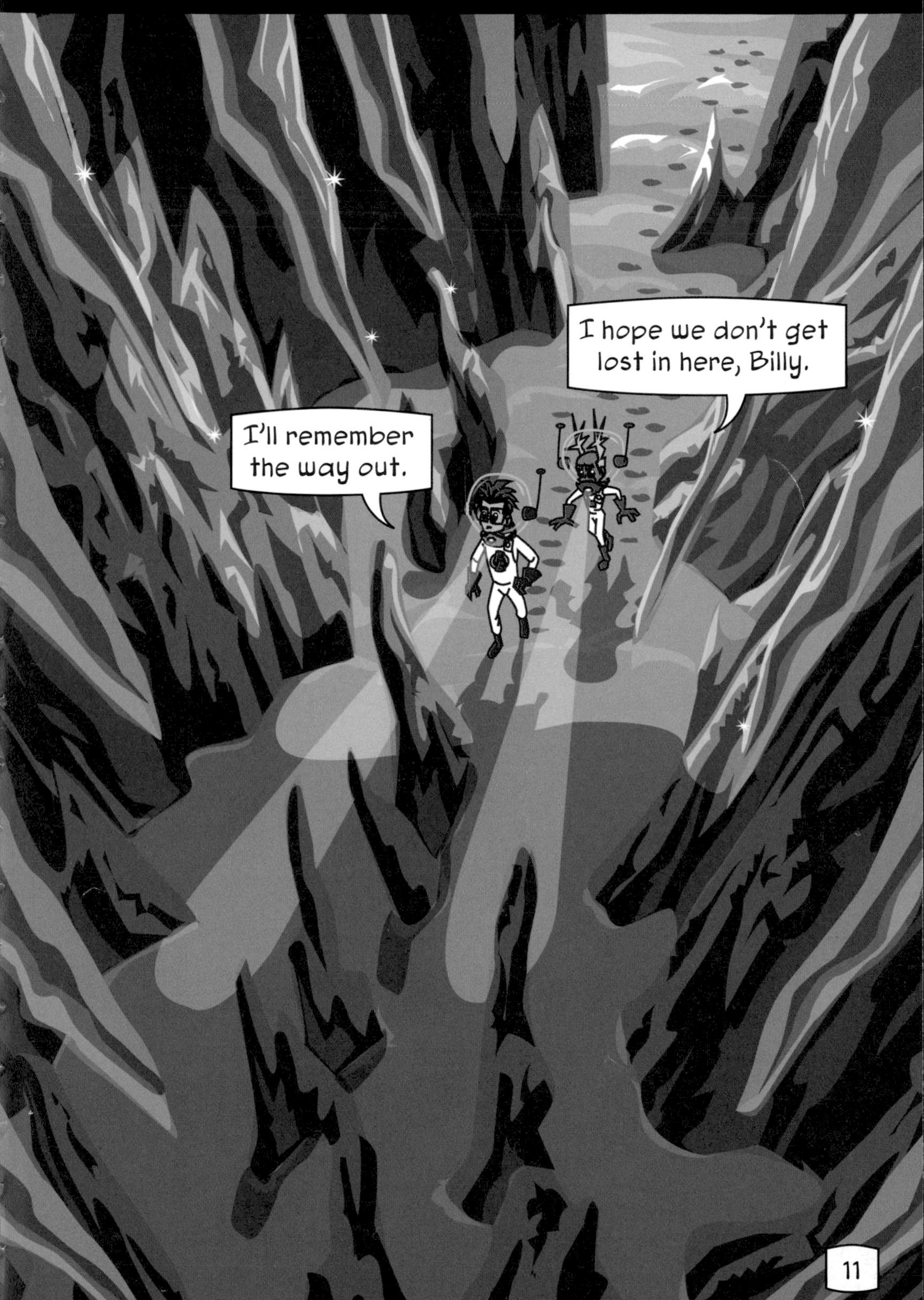
I hope we don't get lost in here, Billy.
I'll remember the way out.

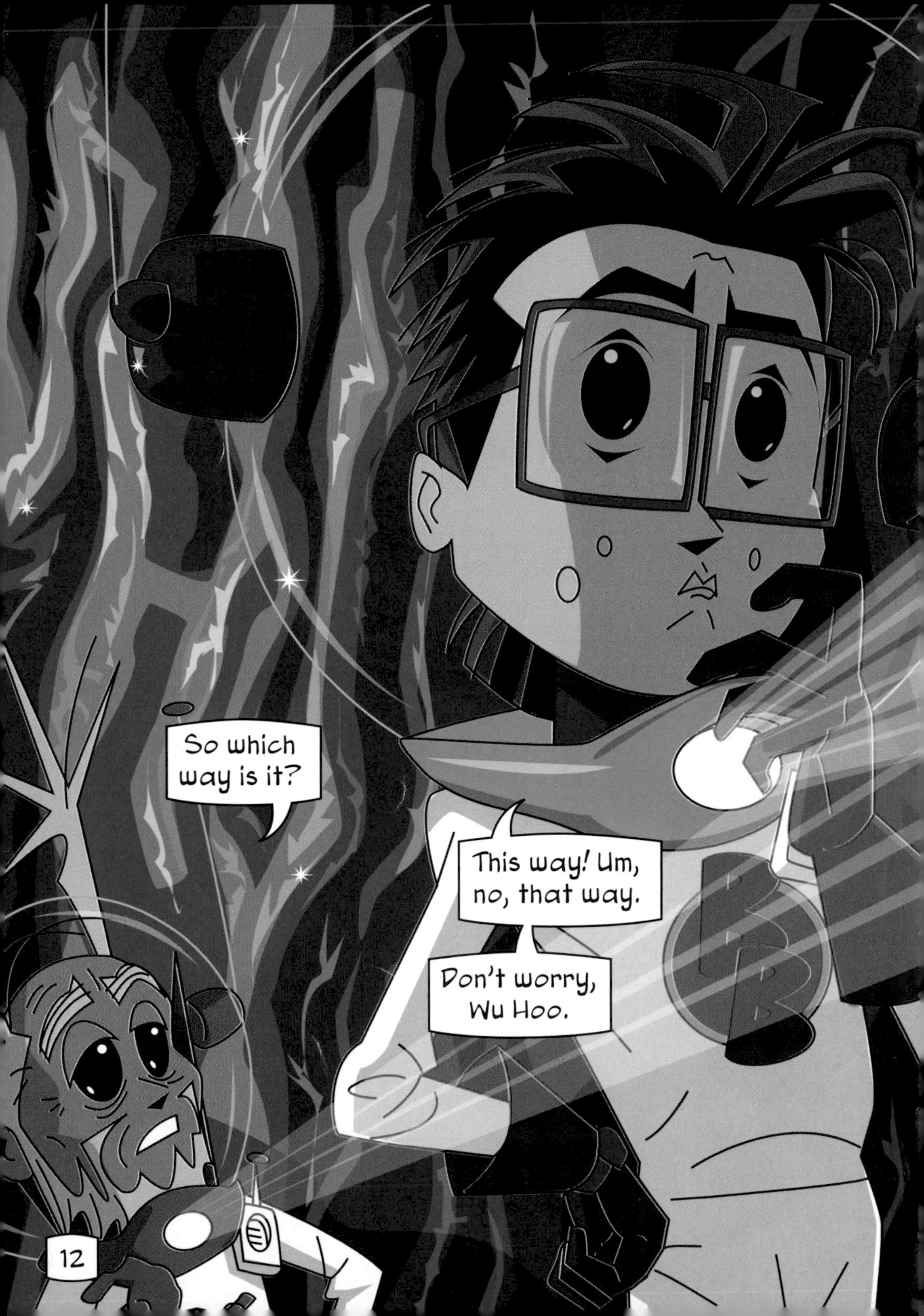
So which way is it?
This way! Um, no, that way.
Don't worry, Wu Hoo.

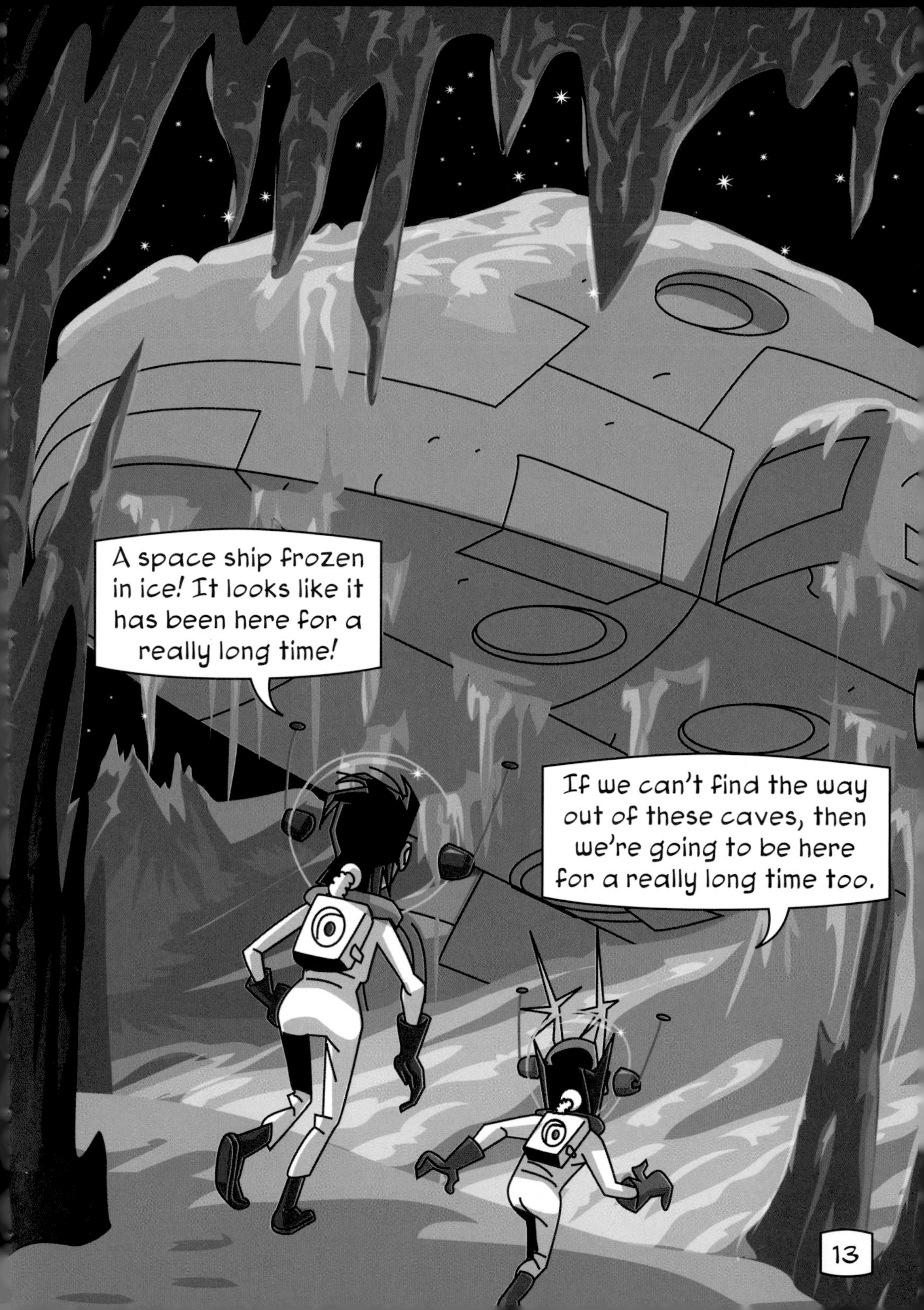
A space ship frozen in ice! It looks like it has been here for a really long time!
If we can't find the way out of these caves, then we're going to be here for a really long time too.

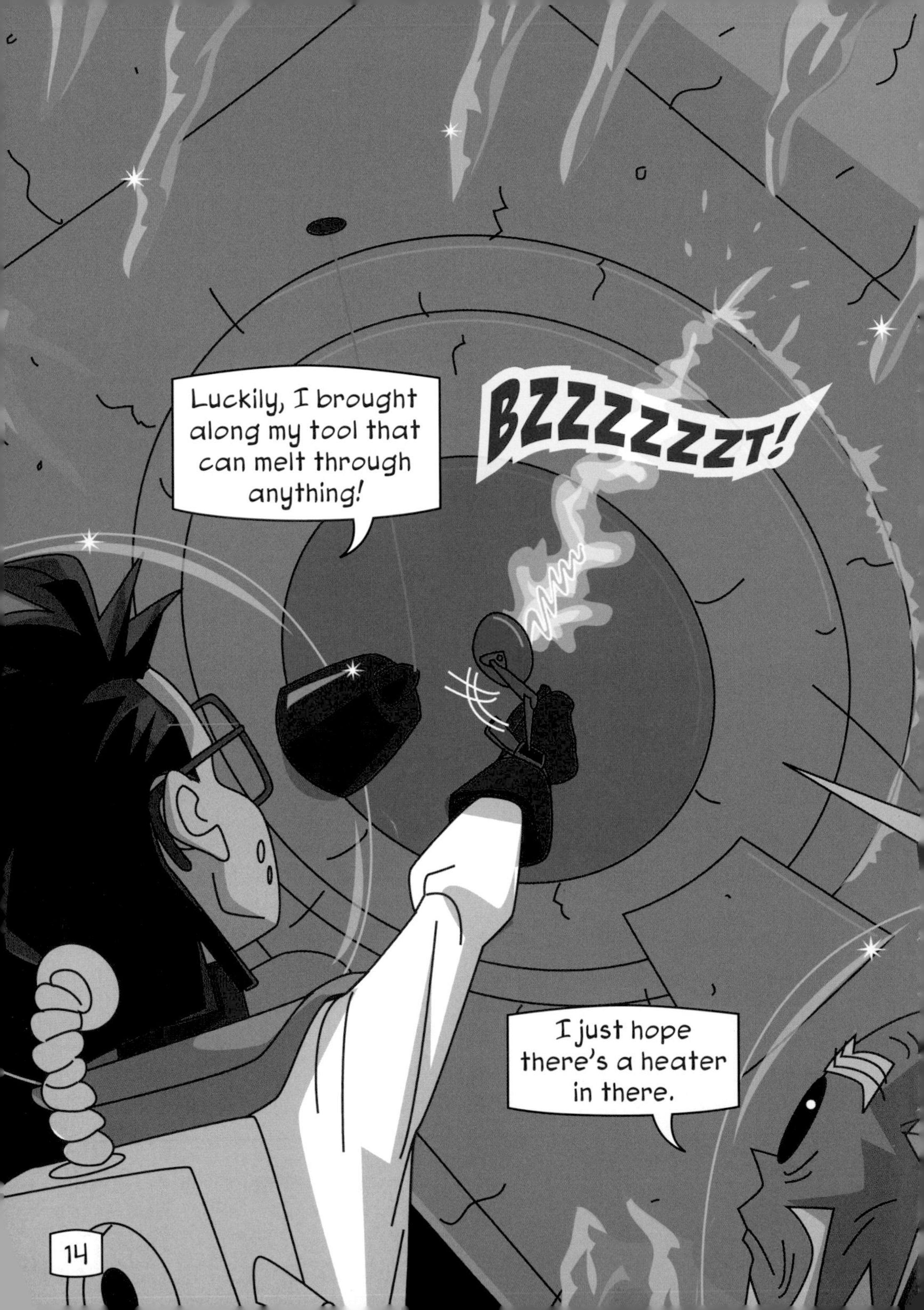
Luckily, I brought along my tool that can melt through anything!
BZZZZZZZT!
I just hope there's a heater in there.

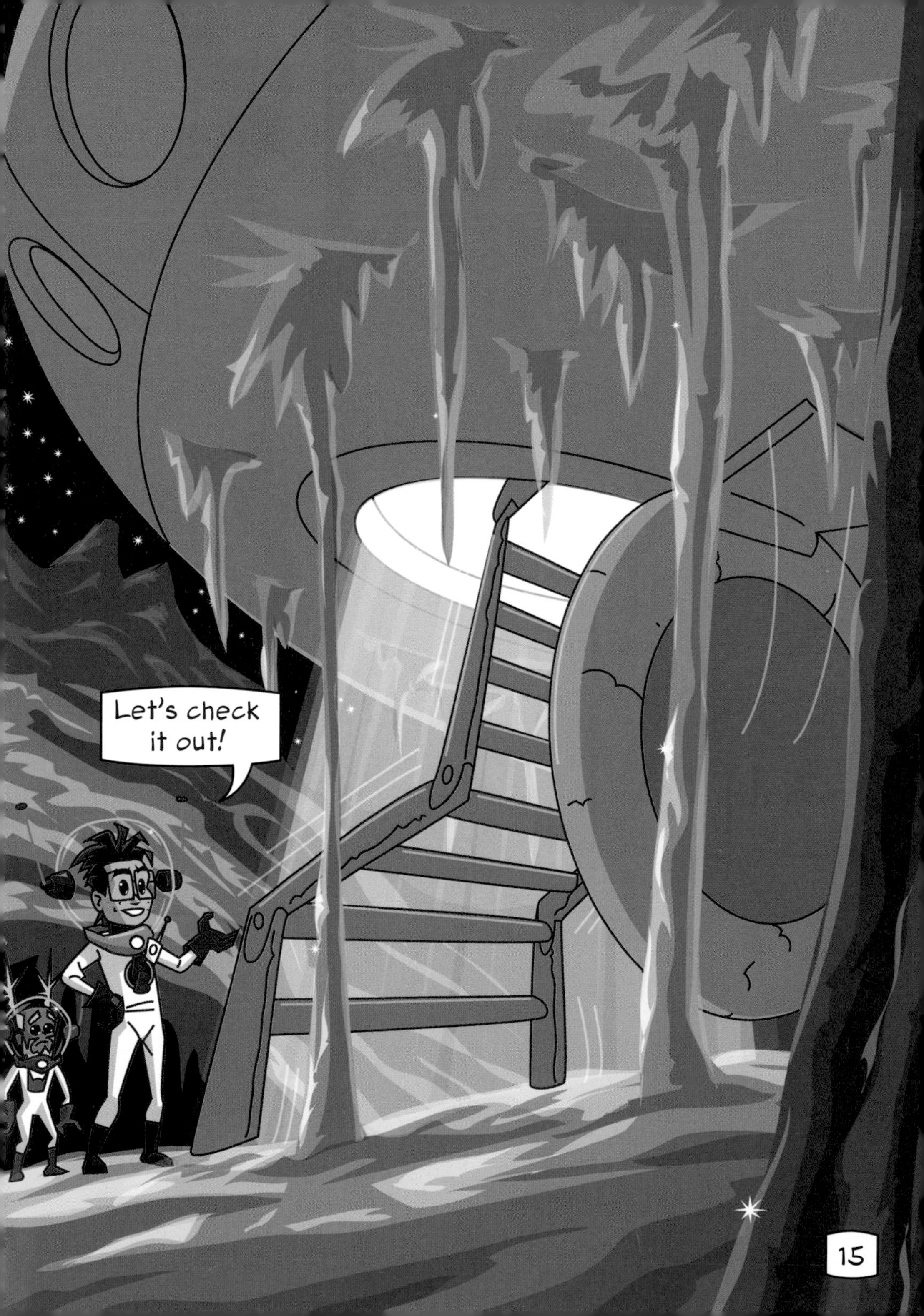
Let's check it out!

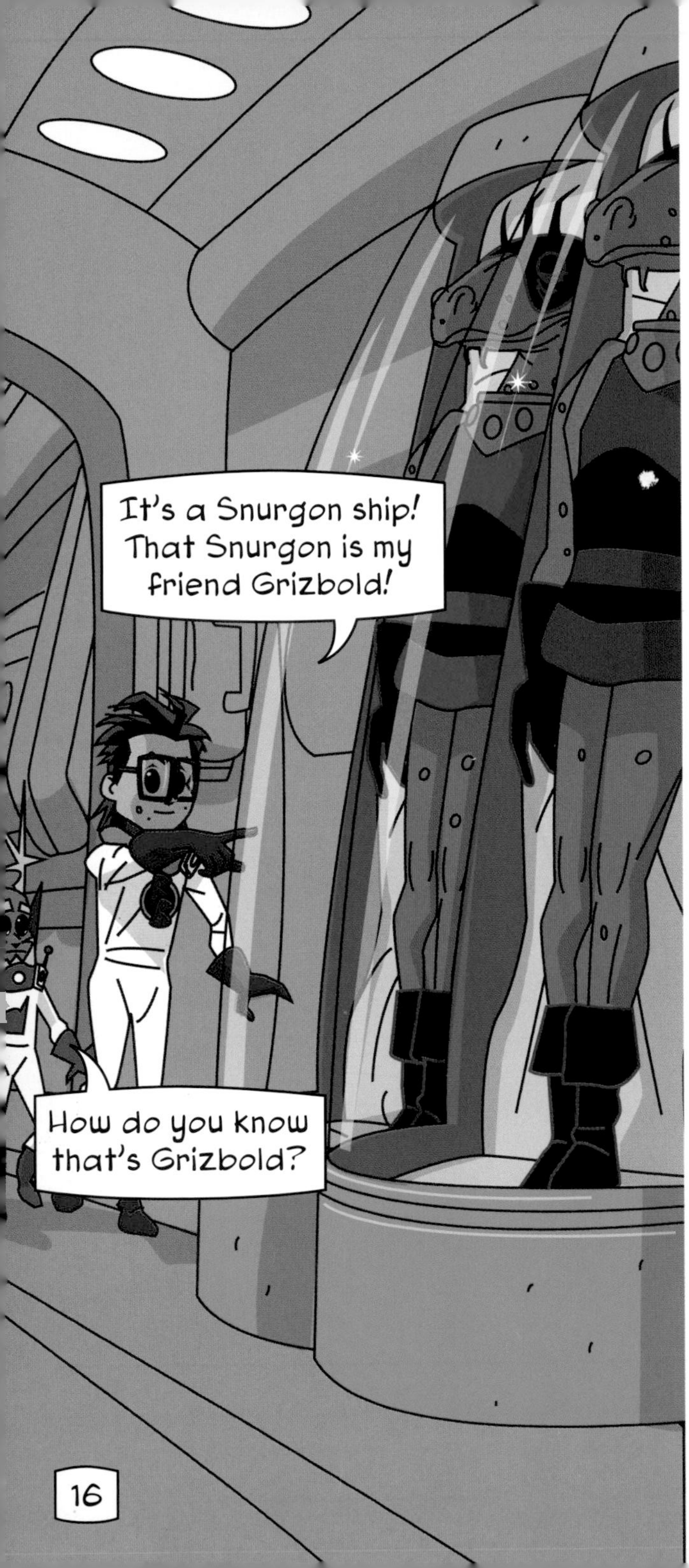
It's a Snurgon ship! That Snurgon is my friend Grizbold!
How do you know that's Grizbold?

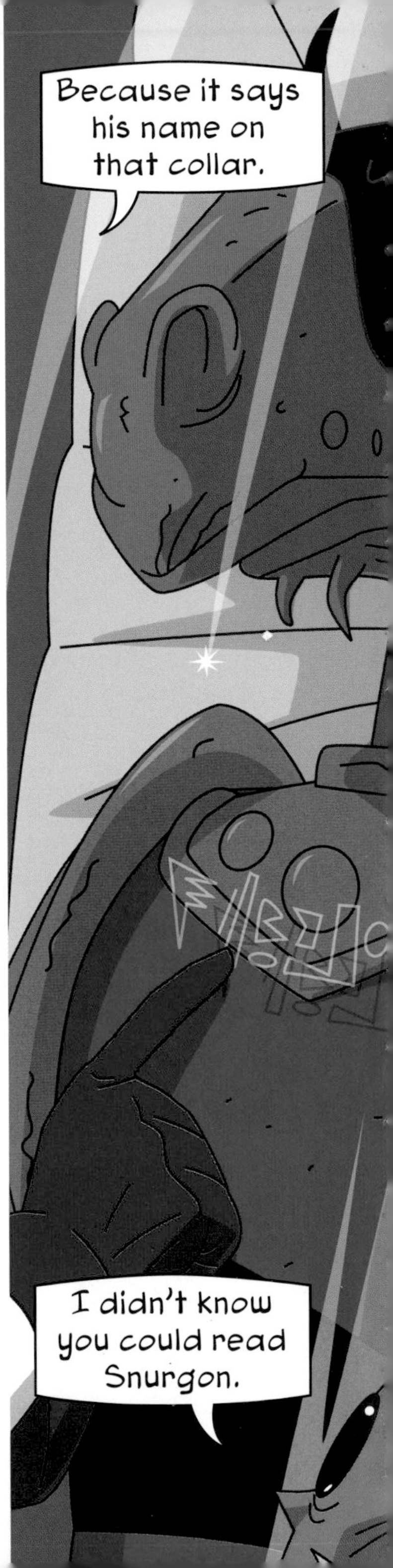
Because it says his name on that collar.
I didn't know you could read Snurgon.

There's a lot about me that you don't know, Wu Hoo.
I'm going to wake them up now. Go make some coffee for them, please?

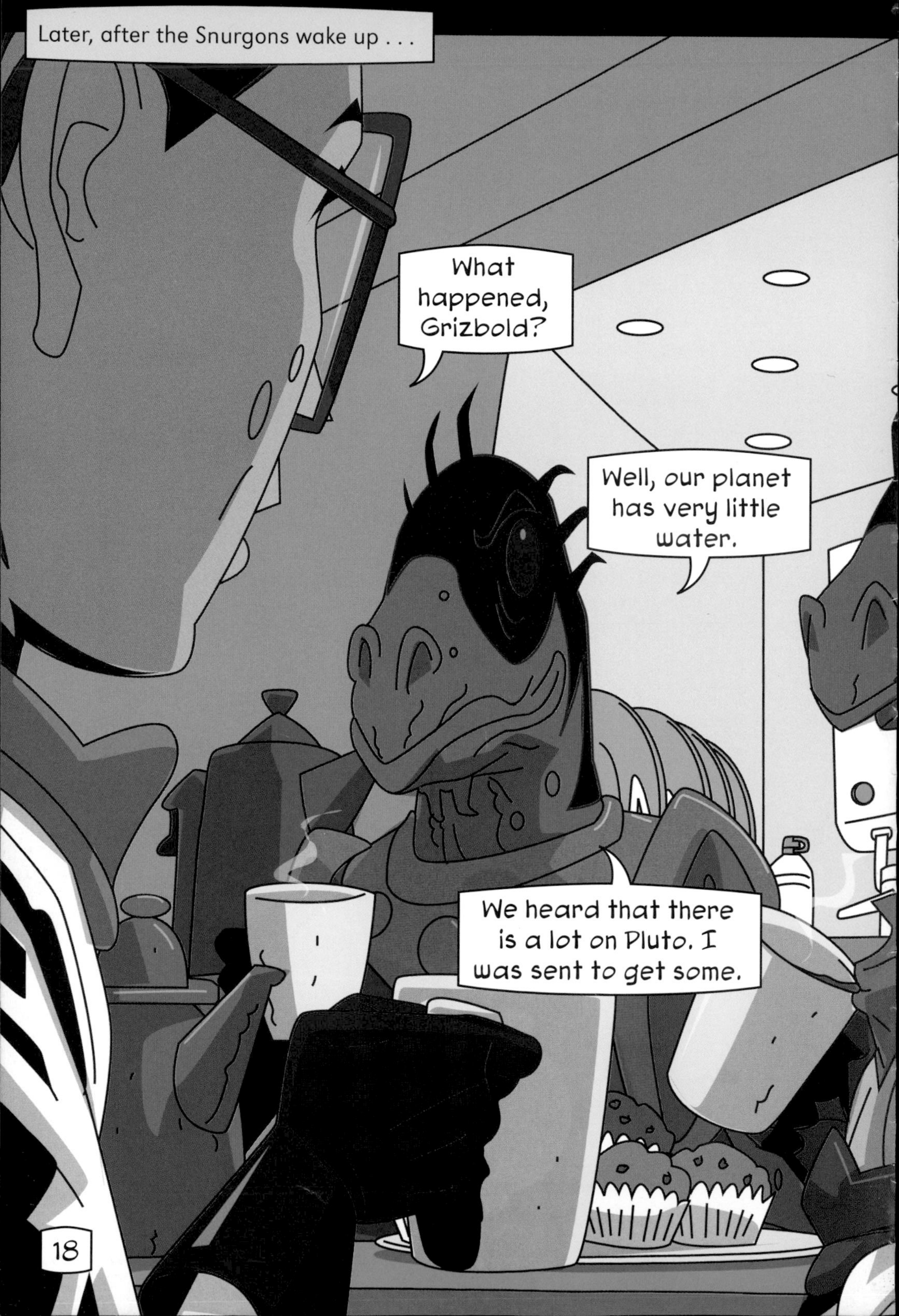
Later, after the Snurgons wake up . . .
What happened, Grizbold?
Well, our planet has very little water.
We heard that there is a lot on Pluto. I was sent to get some.

It is a long trip back, so we decided to take a nap before we went home.
But Snurgons don't sleep for just a few hours. You hibernate for months!

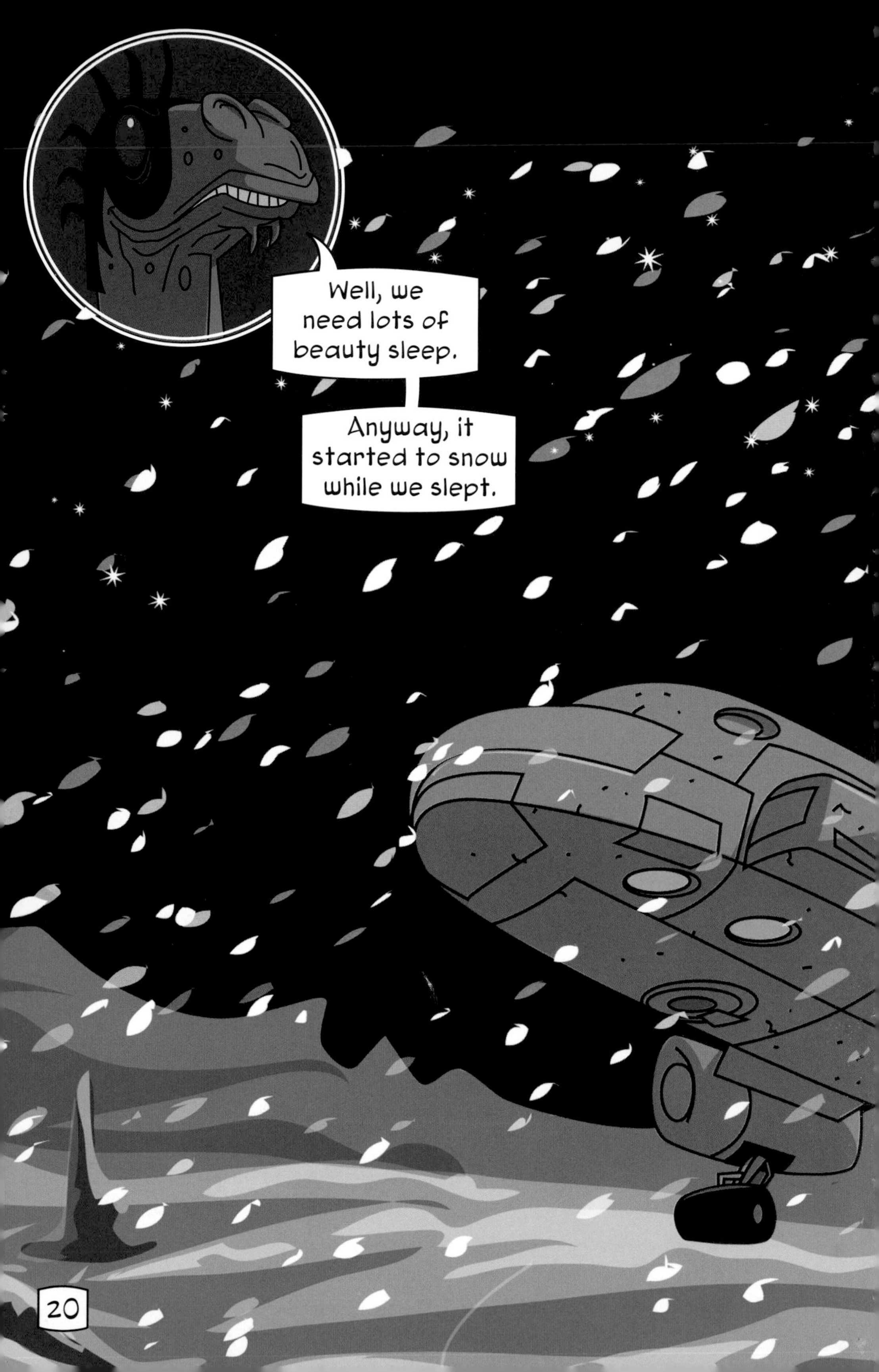
Well, we need lots of beauty sleep.
Anyway, it started to snow while we slept.

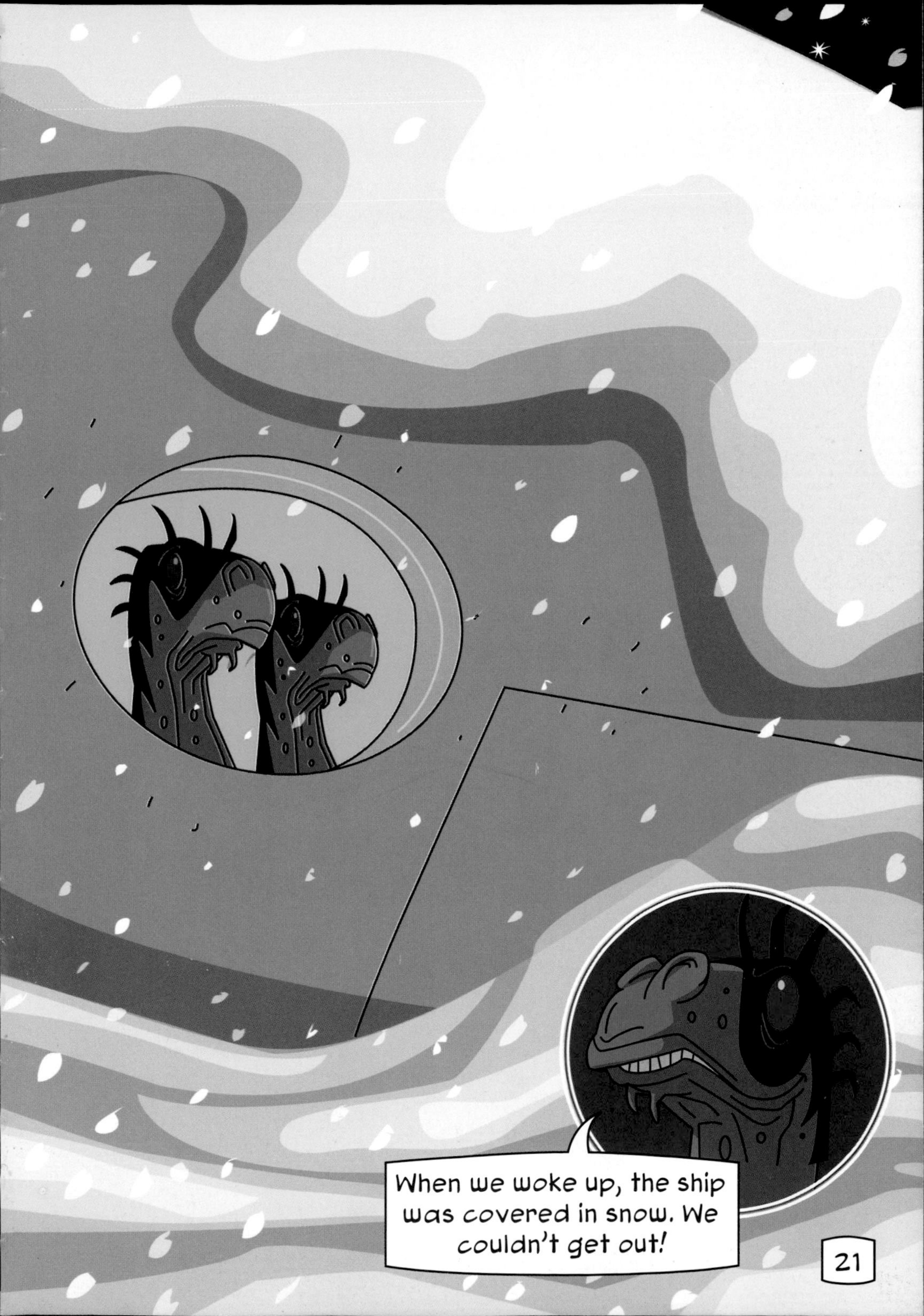
When we woke up, the ship was covered in snow. We couldn't get out!

Good thing we came along, Grizbold!
I have a special new tool on my ship. I can use it to free your ship!
Billy Blaster is great! He's the smartest kid in the whole solar system!

Billy and his friends try to find their way out.

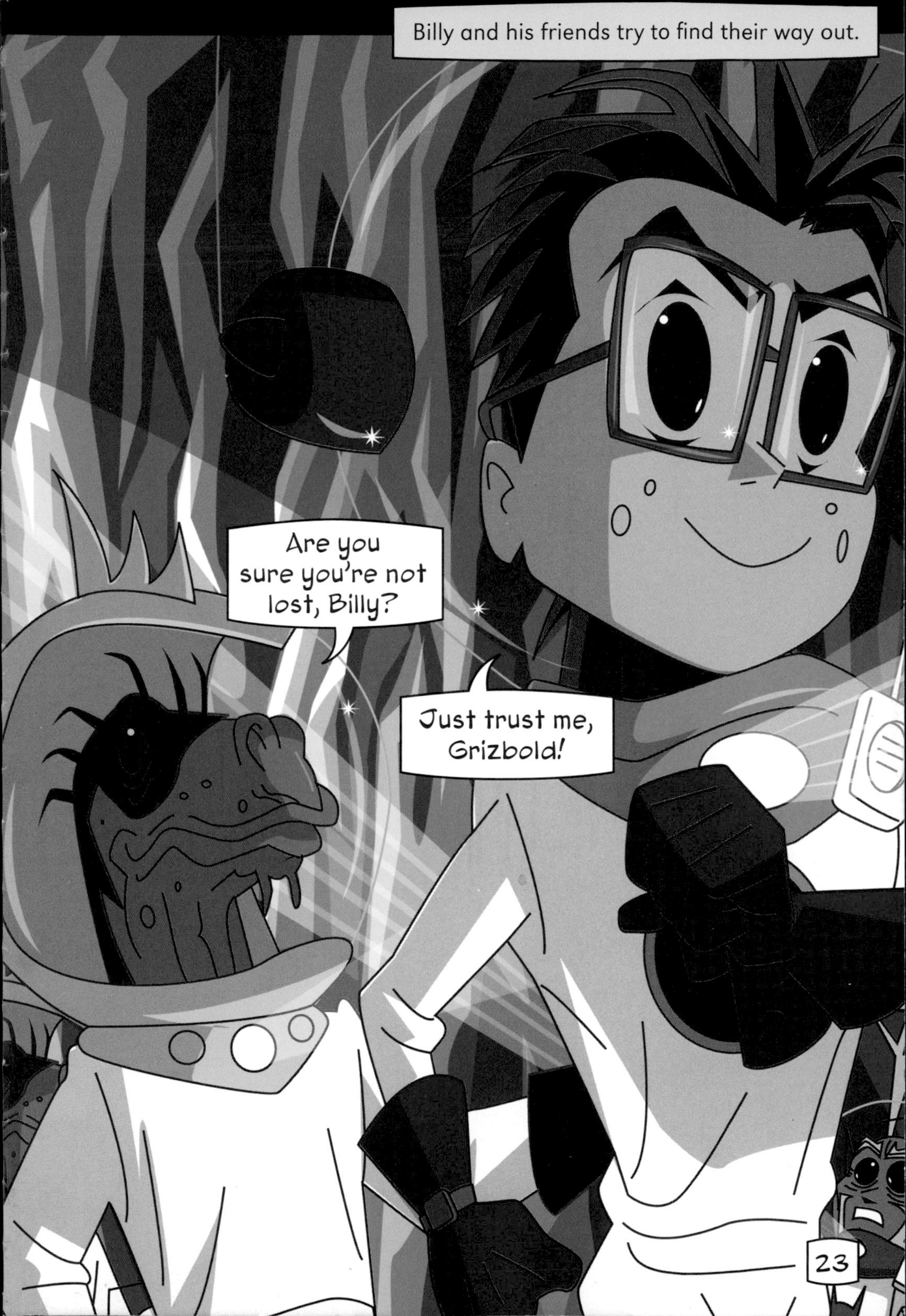
Are you sure you're not lost, Billy?
Just trust me, Grizbold!

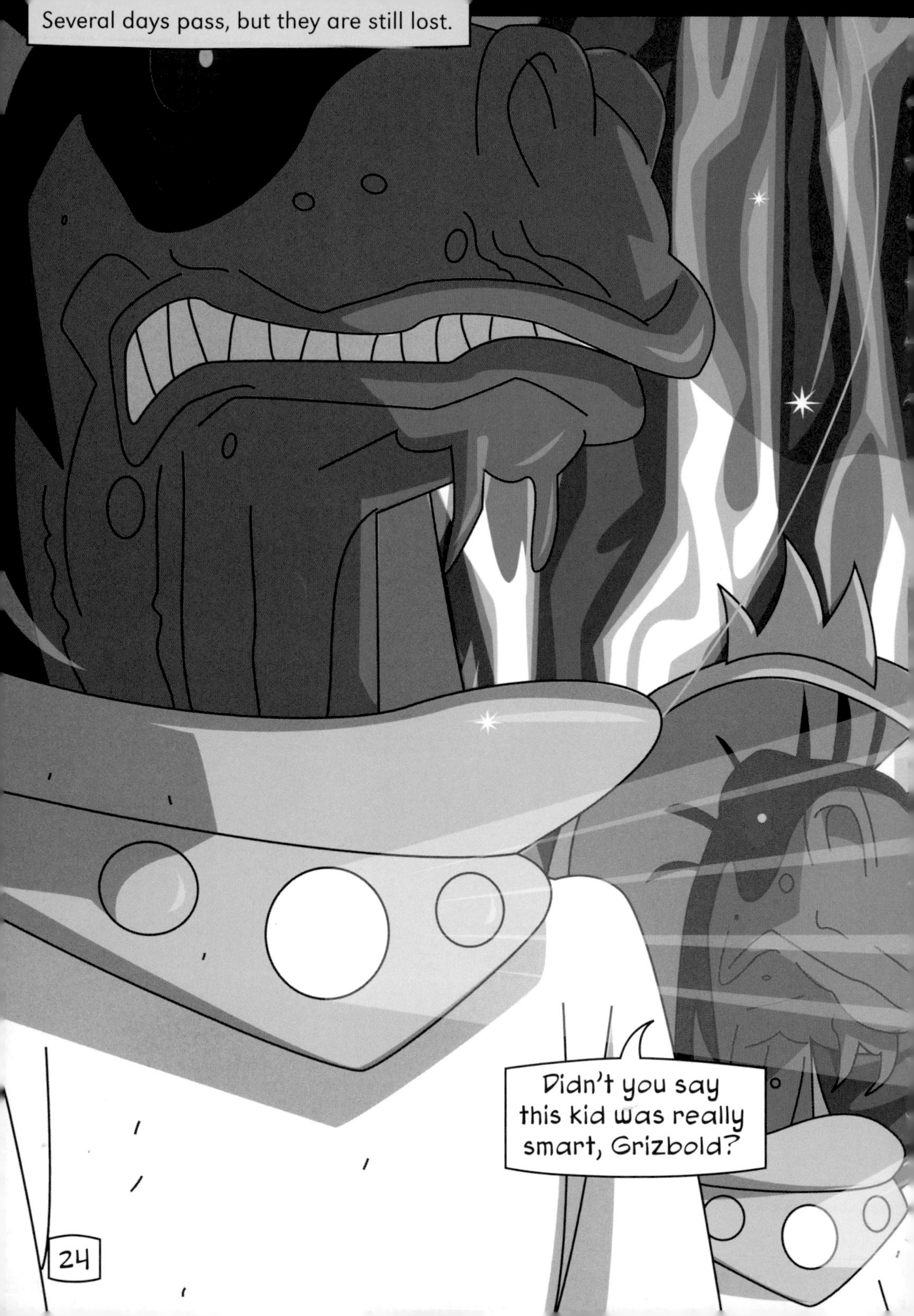
Several days pass, but they are still lost.
Didn't you say this kid was really smart, Grizbold?

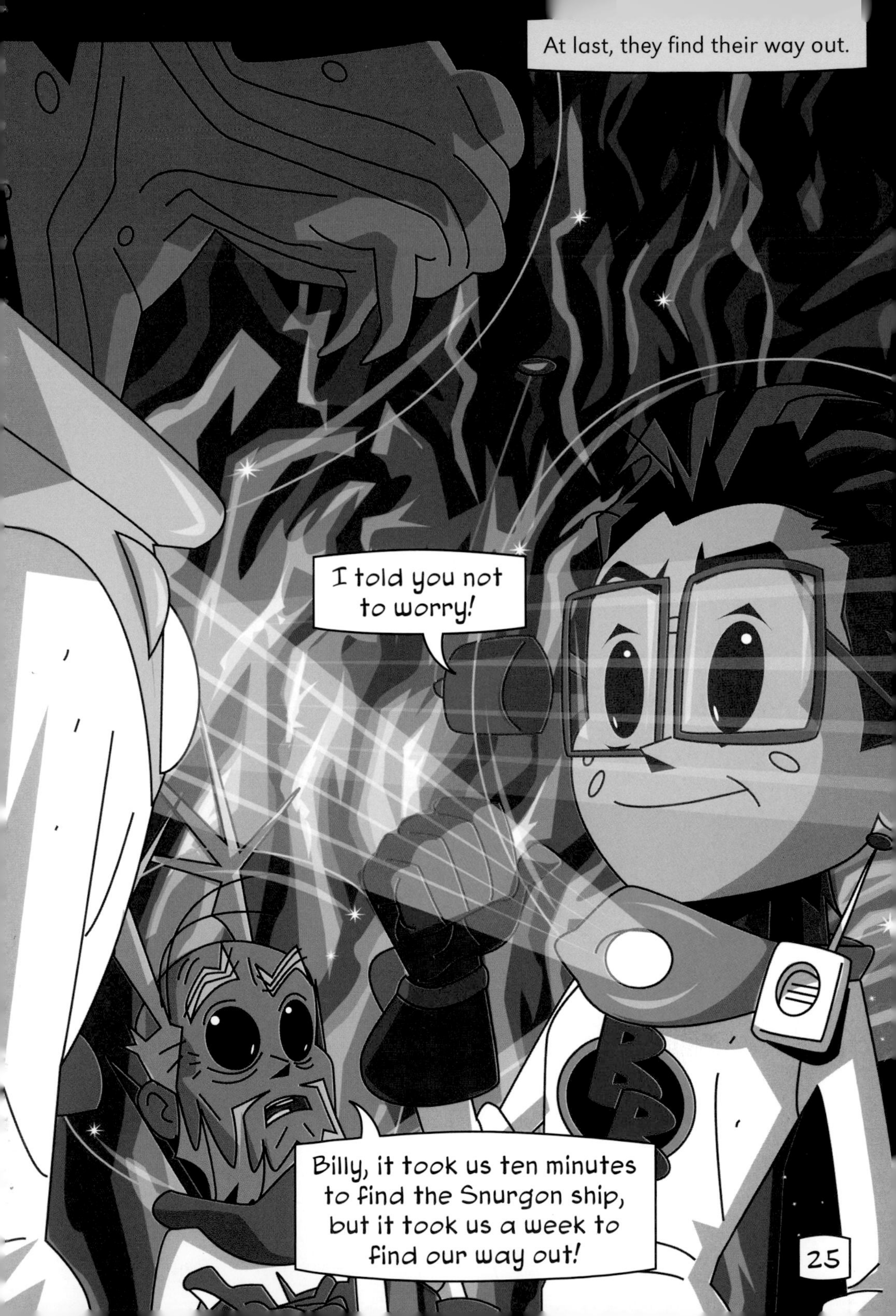
At last, they find their way out.
I told you not to worry!
Billy, it took us ten minutes to find the Snurgon ship, but it took us a week to find our way out!

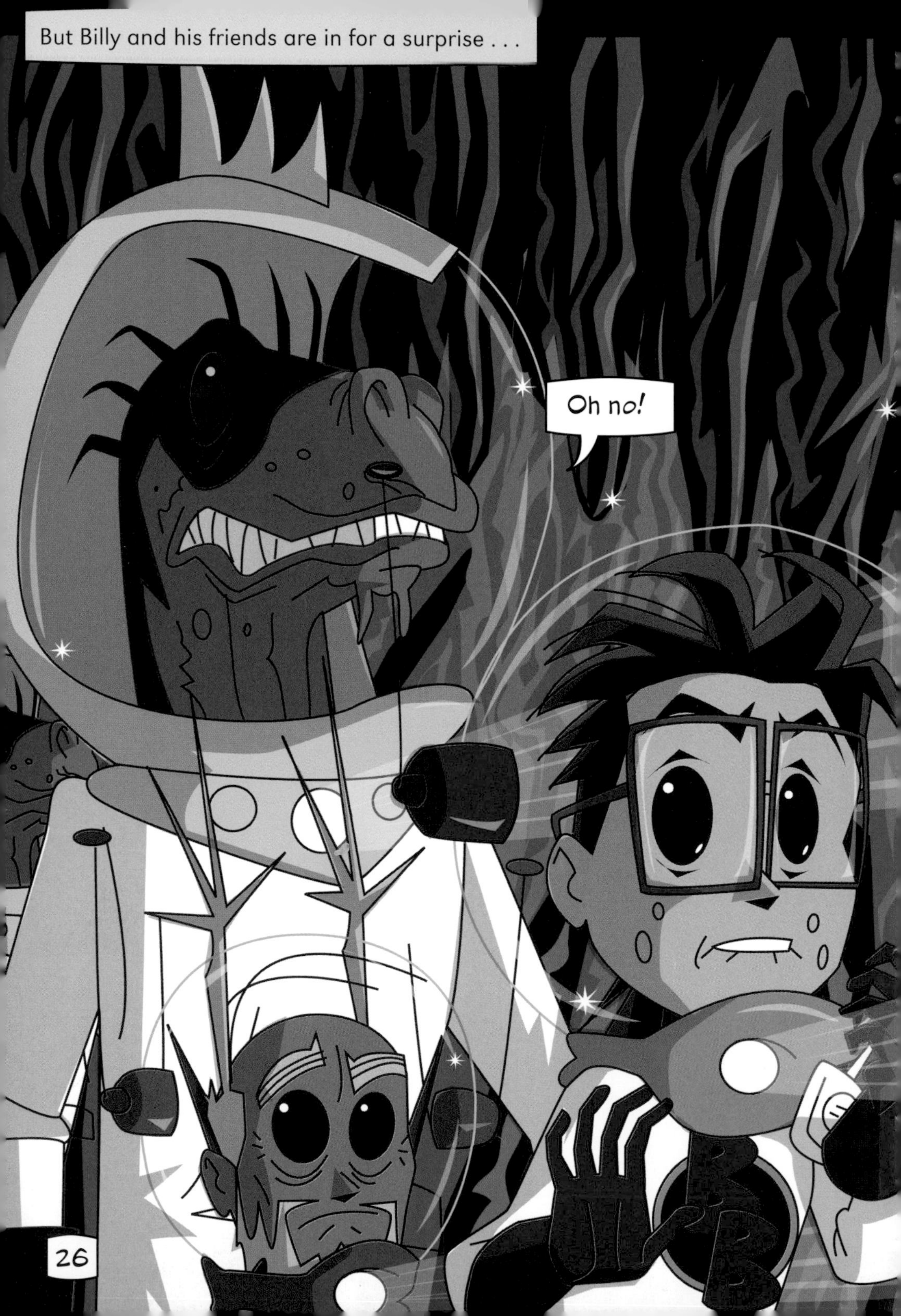
But Billy and his friends are in for a surprise . . .
Oh no!

It snowed again, and Billy's ship is trapped.

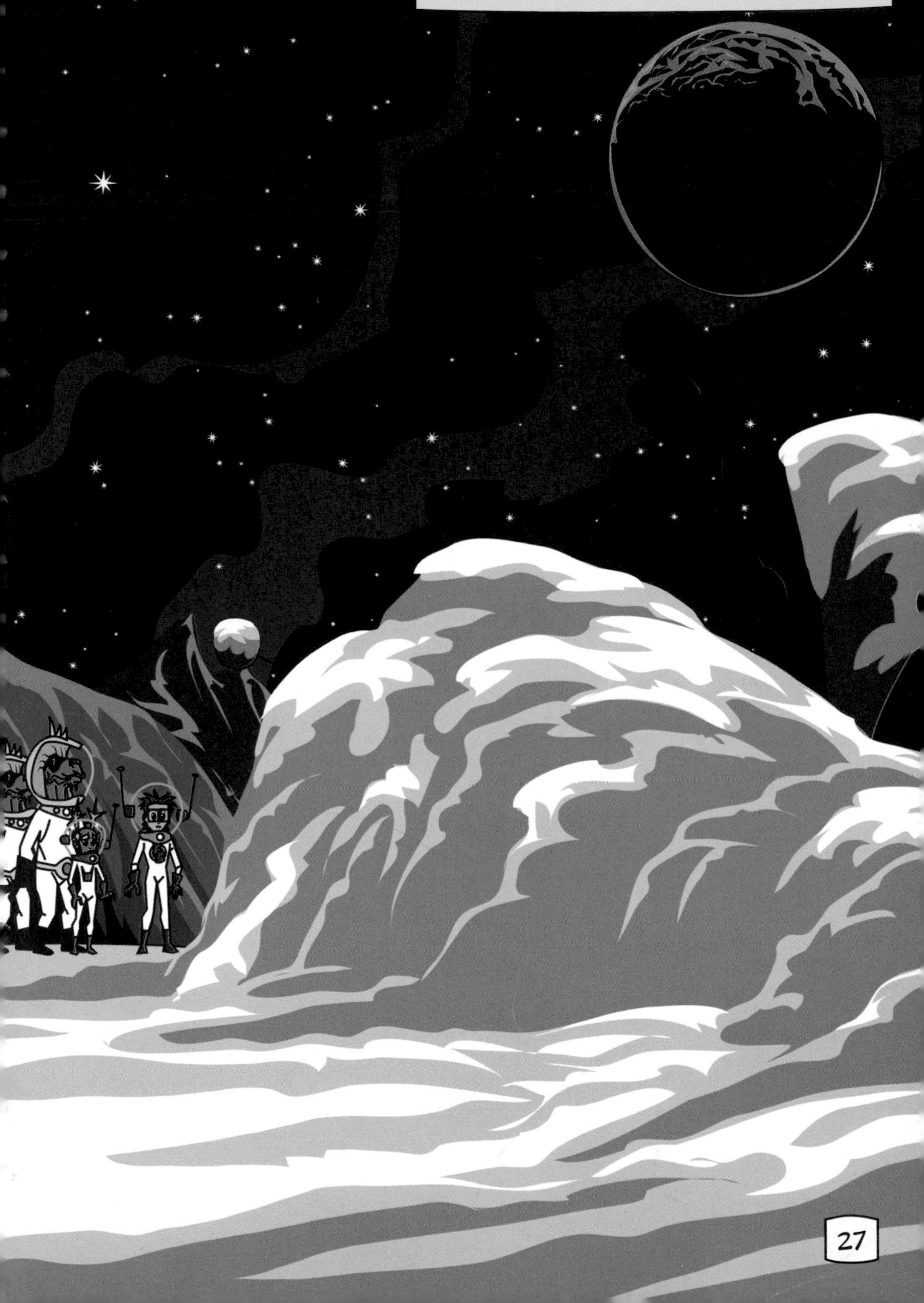

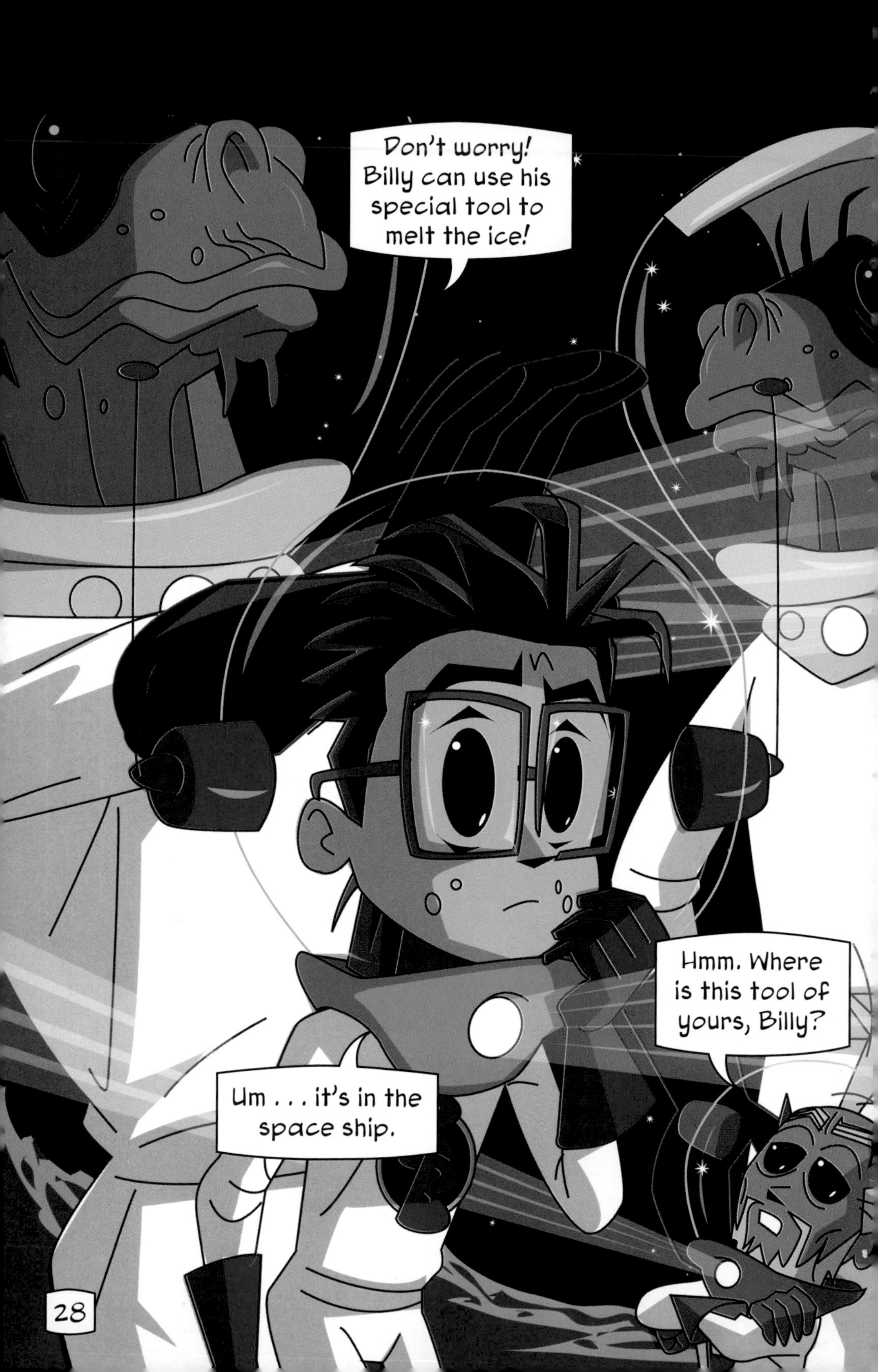
Don't worry! Billy can use his special tool to melt the ice!
Hmm. Where is this tool of yours, Billy?
Um . . . it's in the space ship.

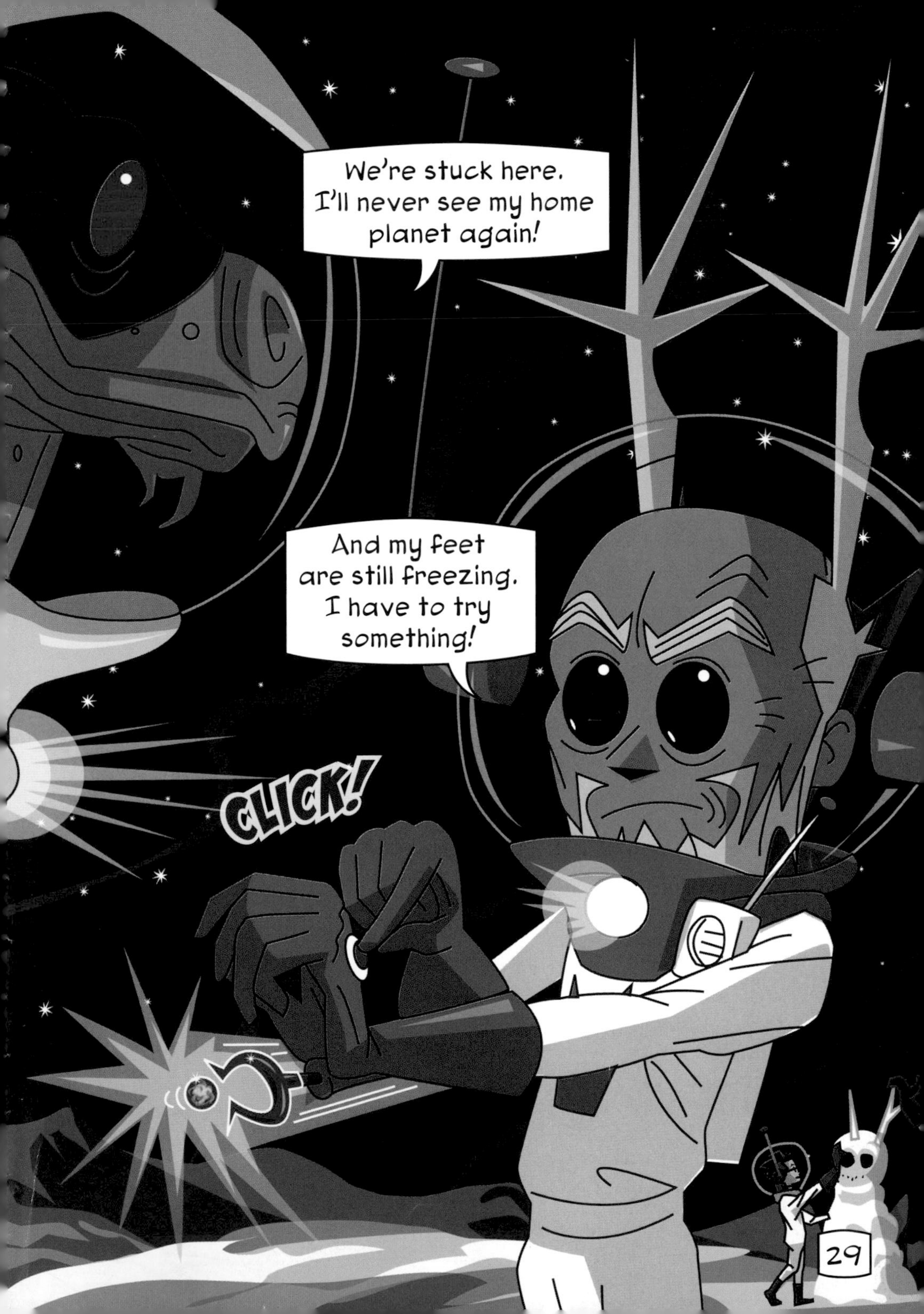
We're stuck here. I'll never see my home planet again!
And my feet are still freezing. I have to try something!
CLICK!

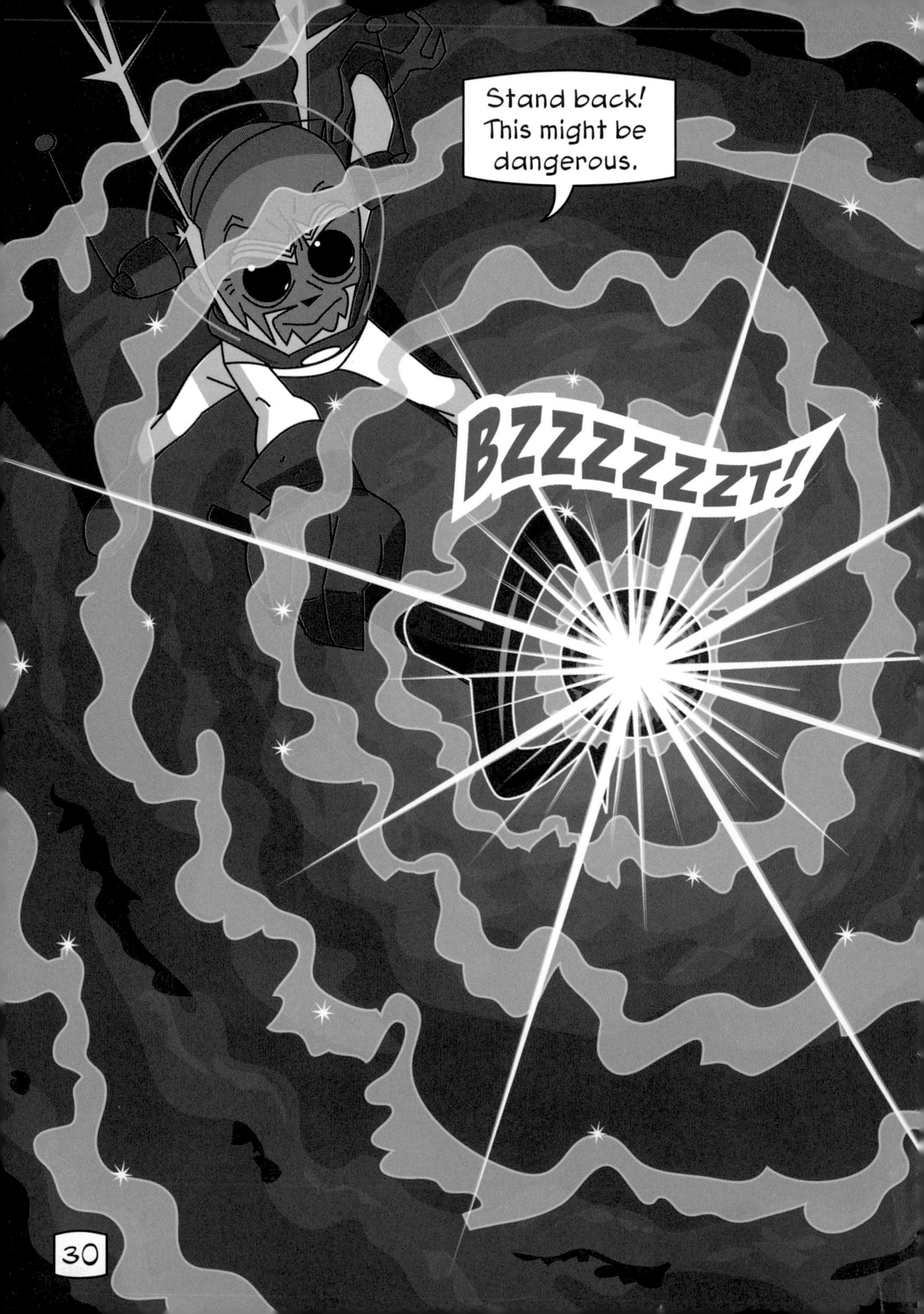
Stand back! This might be dangerous.
BZZZZZZZT!

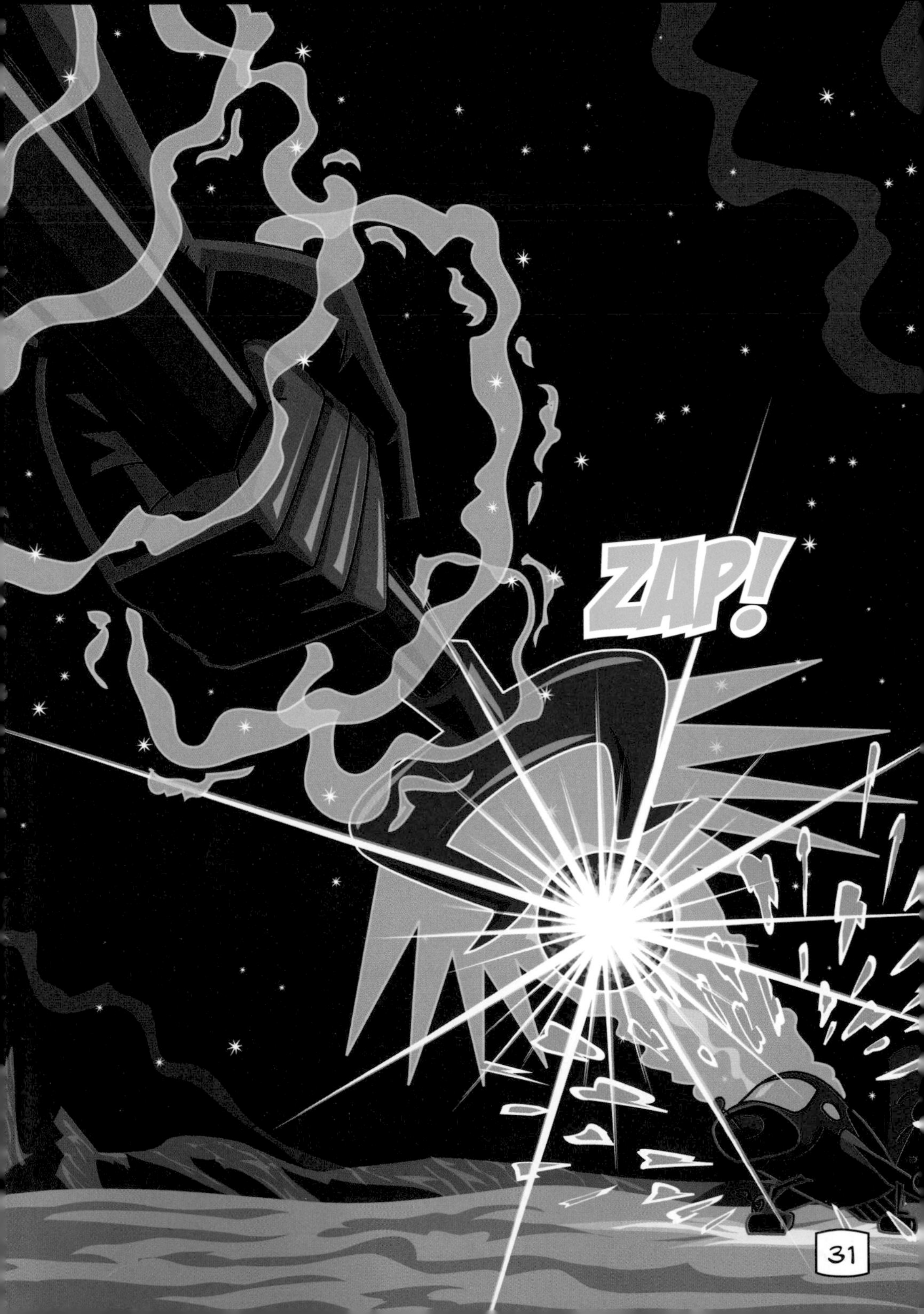
ZAP!

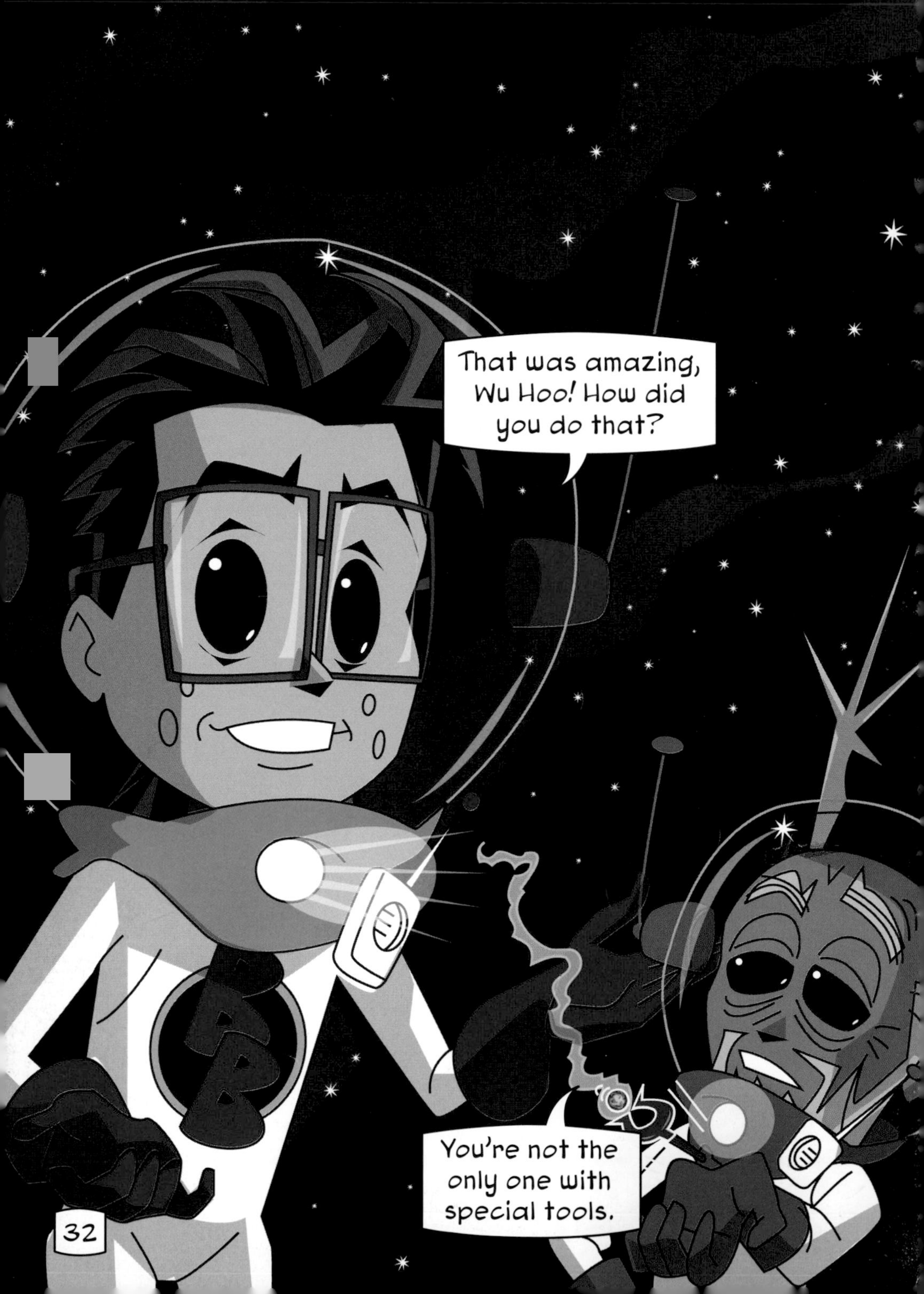
That was amazing, Wu Hoo! How did you do that?
You're not the only one with special tools.

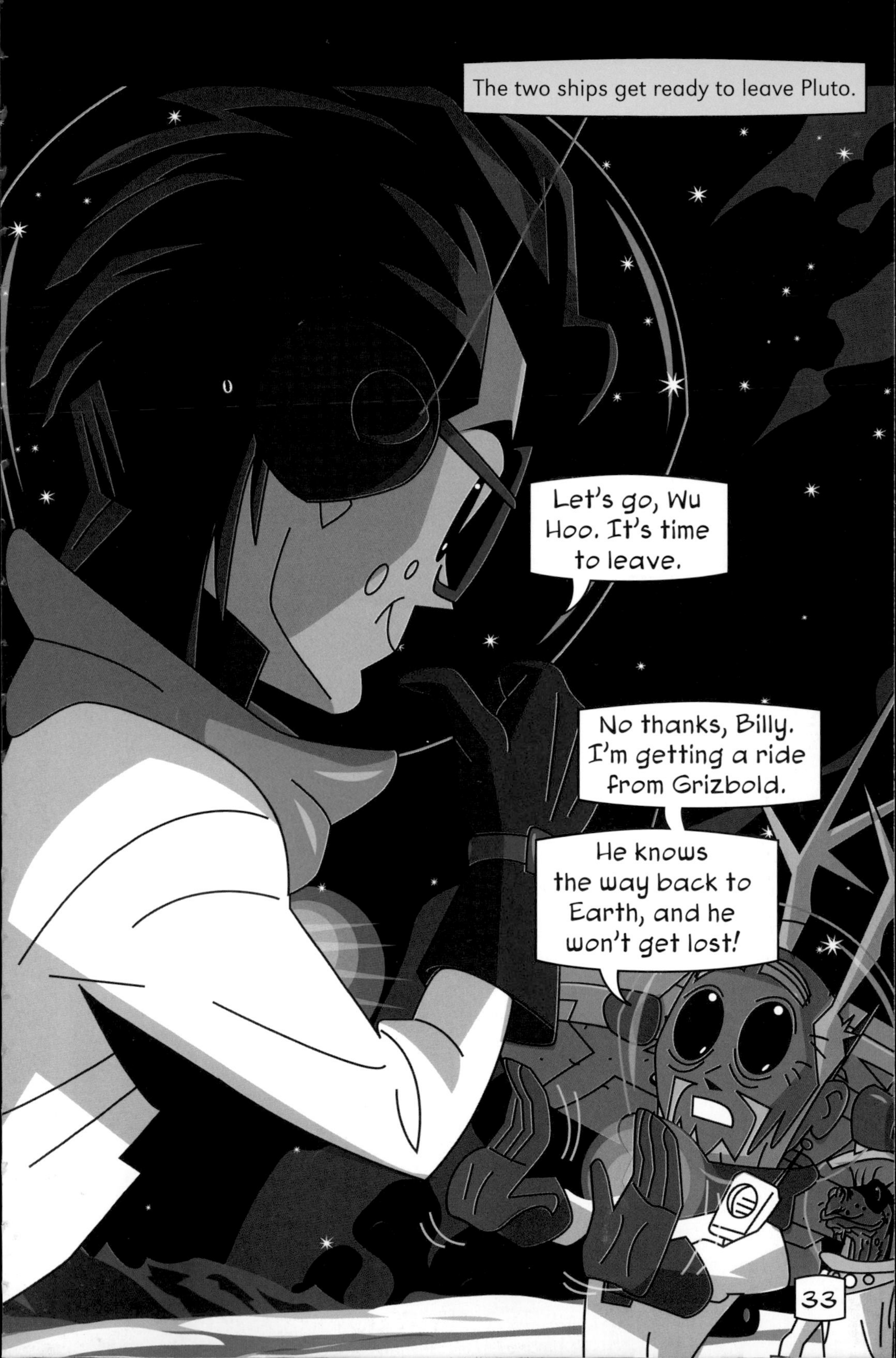
The two ships get ready to leave Pluto.
Let's go, Wu Hoo. It's time to leave.
No thanks, Billy. I'm getting a ride from Grizbold.
He knows the way back to Earth, and he won't get lost!

ABOUT THE AUTHOR

David Orme was a teacher for 18 years before he became a full-time writer. When he is not writing books, he travels around the country, giving performances, running writing workshops, and running courses. David has written more than 250 books, including poetry collections and anthologies, fiction and nonfiction, and school textbooks. He currently lives in Winchester, England.

ABOUT THE ILLUSTRATOR

Peter Richardson's illustrations have appeared in a variety of productions and publications. He has done character designs and storyboards for many of London's top animation studios as well as artwork for advertising campaigns by big companies like BP and British Airways. His work often appears in *The Sunday Times* and *The Guardian*, as well as many magazines. He loves the Billy Blaster books and looks forward to seeing where Billy and his ninja sidekick Wu Hoo will end up next.

GLOSSARY

collar (KOL-ur)—the part of clothing that fits around the neck

dangerous (DAYN-jur-uhss)—likely to cause harm or injury

frozen (FROH-zuhn)—extremely cold, or chilled until hard

hibernate (HYE-bur-nate)—when something hibernates, it goes into a deep sleep for a long time

melt (MELT)—change from solid to liquid by heating

Pluto (PLOO-toh)—Pluto is a dwarf planet. It is the farthest planet from the sun. Pluto is over 2 billion miles from Earth! It's very cold and made of ice.

Snurgons (SNUR-gonz)—lizard-like aliens from a faraway desert planet

solar system (SOH-lur SISS-tuhm)—the sun and the planets that move in orbit around it

strange (STRAYNJ)—different or odd

SLEEPY SNURGONS!

What do the Snurgons have in common with bears, squirrels, rattlesnakes, and bats? They all hibernate!

There is less food available to most animals during the winter. In the fall, animals that hibernate eat a lot of food and store it in their bodies as fat. When winter comes, they have plenty of food and they start to hibernate.

During hibernation, an animal's body temperature, heartbeat, and breathing slow down. Its body uses less energy. That way, it can survive the winter without eating much. It doesn't have to worry about finding food during the winter!

If some animals, like bears, couldn't hibernate during winter, they would be more likely to starve. Hibernation keeps them safe.

Some scientists are trying to find ways for humans to hibernate. They think that humans could be frozen in a very cold container. While frozen, humans would age much slower and would require no food or water. Sick people could be frozen and kept safe until they could be cured!

NASA is interested in freezing humans too. If astronauts could hibernate, they'd be able to visit faraway planets. Otherwise, the trip would be too long and the spaceship wouldn't have enough room for all the food and water the astronauts would need. Also, since they'd be sleeping, the trip wouldn't seem as long!

DISCUSSION QUESTIONS

1. Billy and his friends get lost in the ice caves. Have you ever gotten lost? What happened? Did someone help you? What should you do if you ever get lost?

2. Snurgons hibernate. Hibernation is a deep sleep that lasts through winter. Can you name any other animals that hibernate? If you could hibernate, would you sleep through winter? Do you think animals dream while they hibernate?

3. The Snurgons try to find water to help their home planet. Have you ever done anything to help people where you live? What did you do? What are some ways to help others?

WRITING PROMPTS

1. Pretend you're a Snurgon — a lizard-like alien from another planet. What is your Snurgon name? What do you do for fun? What do you eat? Write about what your day would be like.

2. Billy travels across the solar system. He visits other planets with his sidekick Wu Hoo. If you had a space ship, where would you go? Who would your sidekick be?

3. Wu Hoo and Billy both use special tools to help the Snurgons. Pretend you can make any kind of special tool. What would your tool do? What would you use it for?

INTERNET SITES

Do you want to know more about subjects related to this book? Or are you interested in learning about other topics? Then check out FactHound, a fun, easy way to find Internet sites.

Our investigative staff has already sniffed out great sites for you!

Here's how to use FactHound:

1. Visit *www.facthound.com*

2. Select your grade level.

3. To learn more about subjects related to this book, type in the book's ISBN number: **9781434212757**.

4. Click the **Fetch It** button.

FactHound will fetch the best Internet sites for you!